S0-AYQ-254

This igloo book
belongs to:

....

igloobooks

Written by Melanie Joyce
Illustrated by Steve James

Cover designed by Amy Bradford
Interiors designed by Amy Bradford & Alex Alexandrou
Edited by Kathryn Beer

Copyright © 2018 Igloo Books Ltd

An imprint of Igloo Books Group,
part of Bonnier Books UK
bonnierbooks.co.uk

Published in 2019
by Igloo Books Ltd, Cottage Farm
Sywell, NN6 0BJ
All rights reserved, including the right of reproduction
in whole or in part in any form.

Manufactured in China. GUA009 0519
10 9 8 7 6 5 4 3 2 1

Library of Congress Cataloging-in-Publication
Data is available upon request.

ISBN 978-1-83852-522-4
IglooBooks.com
bonnierbooks.co.uk

There's nobody quite like

Bubblegum Bear.

He's bubble gum pink

and he doesn't care.

Bubblegum isn't like his other bear friends.
He doesn't follow fashion, or keep up with trends.

Bubblegum Bear
can't dance, or sing. . .

. . . but that doesn't matter,
he just does his own thing.

And although his voice makes a terrible sound, everyone cheers and cries,

Bubblegum Bear doesn't worry at all,
that he can't swing a racket, or score with a ball.

It doesn't bother him that he can't run fast,
and at the end of a race is usually last.

Because Bubblegum Bear
just likes taking part.

Whatever he does,
he gives it his heart.

And if things don't work out, well that is okay.

Bubblegum Bear won't let it spoil his day.

Big, swirly slide

If it's cloudy and dull, with rain pouring down,
Bubblegum Bear won't grumble or frown.

He'll put on his boots to play outside,
and all his friends follow to the big, swirly slide.

Bubblegum Bear never has any doubt,
that after the rain, the sun will come out.

He'll pack up some snacks and go on a hike. . .

. . . or maybe whizz off on his shiny red bike.

Bubblegum Bear is as happy as can be,
acting like a pirate, sailing out to sea!

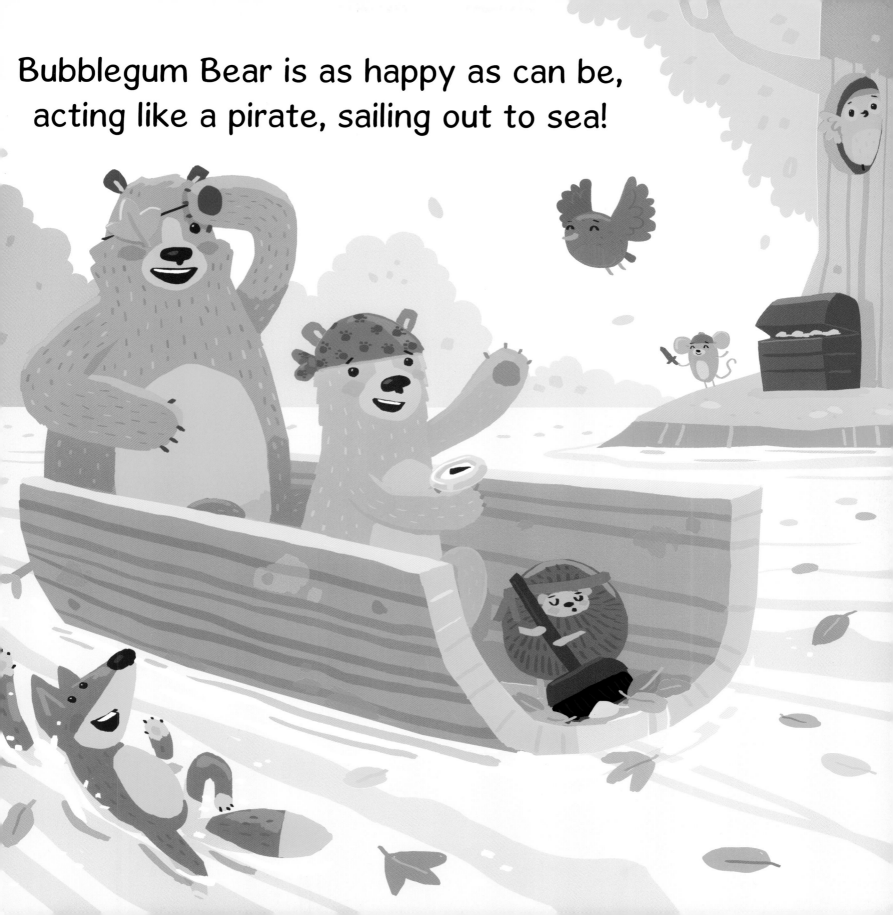

They have so much fun playing happily together.

His friends think he is the best bear ever.

Because Bubblegum cares
and is always kind, too.
So everyone says,

Bubblegum Bear always does his best, and at the end of the day when it's time to rest...

. . . he sleeps peacefully because there is no one to compare,

with the **loving,** **cuddly, pink** Bubblegum **Bear.**